ELEVEN DAYS 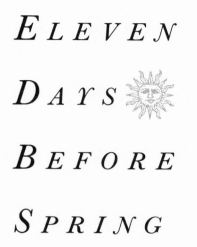 BEFORE SPRING

ELEVEN

DAYS

BEFORE

SPRING

Poems by

JOELLEN KWIATEK

HarperPerennial

A Division of HarperCollins*Publishers*

HarperCollins books may be purchased for educational, business, or sales promotional use. For information, please write: Special Markets Department, HarperCollins Publishers, Inc., 10 East 53rd Street, New York, NY 10022.

FIRST EDITION

Designed by George J. McKeon

Library of Congress Cataloging-in-Publication Data

Kwiatek, JoEllen, 1957–
    Eleven days before spring : poems / by JoEllen Kwiatek.—1st ed.
        p.   cm.
    ISBN 0-06-055350-2—ISBN 0-06-095015-3 (pbk.)
    I. Title.   II. Title: 11 days before spring.
    PS3561.W48E43   1994
    811'.54—dc20   94-9369

94 95 96 97 98 CC/HC 10 9 8 7 6 5 4 3 2 1
94 95 96 97 98 CC/HC 10 9 8 7 6 5 4 3 2 1 (pbk.)

For my sisters

*"But I suppose I still cling
too much to possession and cannot
achieve measureless poverty,
much as that is probably my crucial task."*

—RAINER MARIA RILKE

CONTENTS

PART THREE

ACKNOWLEDGMENTS

Some of these poems first appeared in other magazines, to whose editors grateful acknowledgment is made:

The American Poetry Review: "Field in November," "On the Way to Tell My Sister," "Still Life of the Martyrdom of St. Serapion."

The Antioch Review: "A Painting by Vermeer."

The Indiana Review: "August," " 'Nearer God, Nearer Realité.' "

Pushcart Prize XVIII: The Best of the Small Presses: " 'Nearer God, Nearer Realité' " was reprinted.

For their criticism and encouragement, deepest thanks to Paul Aviles, Karen Fish, Aida Khalil, Sheila Gillooly, and Edward Ruchalski.

ELEVEN DAYS 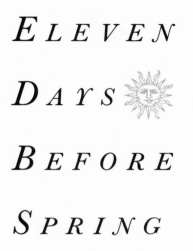 BEFORE SPRING

PART ONE

THE DAYDREAM OF ART HISTORY

for Paul and Aida

Choir blue, flint blue, blue of shards, of
incompleteness, of a distant portion of Italian
    sky
inflated above a spectacle of agony or meditation; if
agony, then a dark oily woods behind
a spotlight clearing where a figure kneels leaning
over a rock for prie-dieu, *or* a grotto desolate
as a glacier, the terraced hillsides far
above it a glacial green, the color of the spring
horizon at twilight when it glows transparent as
an invalid's forehead, the figure in this
case, tiny, harried, caught off guard
as though having just run beyond his doorframe
to find whatever prankster rang the bell vanished
like a daylight star. . . .

                  So temptation vanishes
or is vanquished by the chaste one
in whose mouth it leaves behind a taste of delicious
loss, like the feeling on the back of the neck when
his hair was shorn. His agony cools to meditation.

In the faces of the damned you can see the fits
and starts of agony which moves in place inside

them like a flame. They live eternity by the minute.
But here in this room where the book lies
open and forgotten on the table
or, a forefinger clamped between its pages,
dangles against the long draped thigh of the reader
who like Eve has tasted and now in his mind
wanders dazed or impassioned among fallen leaves
time is different. It's the golden
acre stilled by heat beyond the small square window
positioned high and off center in the wall
like a hand-mirror someone else is holding for you.
It's the time it takes for the lopsided pear
to roll unnoticed to the ledge of the plate and
stay there . . . the false continuity of bees,
their droning that always stops before you stop
hearing it, then the silence afterwards like a breeze
of origins sudden and mysterious. For a moment

longer, you don't move. Meditation is a dip alone in a pool.
A farmhouse shaded by a windbreak of pine, its rooms so
tall & cool they can be walked through as though they were
empty. You draw yourself up & out of the water, your body
following heavily after you. Listen . . .

                              You can hear the wingbeats

in certain self-portraits—the eyes an edifice, a stoic
crumbling remaining wall against them. Moments of dread
do that. Confuse the instant with long ago, memory
arriving as a premonition. Eons & minutes
agonized in the room, though the hands remain unburdened
in the lap, the gaze suspended like a word already spoken
rippling out of the frame, an endless oncoming dying

wave. Every look exceeds its grasp. The blush darkens
on four nectarines
in a stone-blue bowl pitched on a tabletop near the heavy
book of masterpieces—don't turn the page. The Dutch
aren't afraid. They know the cycle repeats itself while
the general population isn't looking. See
above their heads, a giant V of geese moving like a bellows
over the dry hills and fields, pumping oxygen into the fire
of spring.

NATIVITY

for Mary Jo

A fine agitation
detonates the garden.

It is spring
or a thaw heralding spring.

The ground is mottled
turf & snow.

Live weeds
sprout near a border

with the well-behaved
gaiety of sprigs.

The choir members
stand neatly together

fitted as the pleats
of an accordion.

From their mouths
as from far away

issue the trills
of melting snow.

Not one of them
looks toward the baby

exposed
on a wrap by their feet.

They have inner lives
instead, a way of being

there like the membrane
of water: permeable,

deflective.
The other adults

in the garden look
in their beautiful clothes

as unexpected &
delightful as parlor

furniture under a tree.
This mixing of things

is at once ceremonial
& impromptu.

Like the magpie
alighted on the crumbling

lean-to, his profile
coinstruck as a general's.

From this distance
the meaning comes & goes

peacefully
like the noise of a stream

(now you hear it, now you
don't). What could

they all be thinking—
that in spring sometimes

the air responds like
flesh?

LETTING GO

All day the sky
has stayed the color
of a withered leaf,
and now the light
we didn't see was there
begins its slow collapse
across the field:

the trees stiffen
into gesture,
then the low hills
step back—

as though brevity
anticipated loss and
not death.

       Yesterday
we dreamt of a thaw:
out of the black field
the damp air shuddering
like flanks of a horse.

FIELD IN NOVEMBER

The sun stalls
along field stubble,
light broken
by what it must fall on—
weed-scratch, the dry
poke of stalk. A killdeer turns
in its skin.

The horizon shrivels
to a stick
that breaks under my gaze: I
think of waste-places, the desert's
edge, and the slow
grin of a cow's ribs.

"NEARER GOD, NEARER REALITÉ"

—Gwen John

I'm safe—safe in a mood.
The quiet of trees after snowfall
is in my room. The same
sterling expectancy. I
could read now or sew.
Occasionally look up.
To read is to lower
oneself into time as if it were
a bath. I believe
in slowness, in the loss that
precedes harmony.

Listen! if I paint a thing
over and over, it's
not for security or to show
faith: the only way
in for me is to repeat my subject
endlessly, like a chant. (Once

against the pressure of aloneness
I thought the friezework
on the church had the momentum of a herd—
the saints like young bulls with their heads down.)

11

Each weekday I travel from
my room to my studio and
back. On Saturdays I ride
the trams, sketching.
Sundays I go to mass.
To tame my happiness I sleep.

THE LOST FARM

for Edward Ruchalski

In the photograph it is spring. Shadows
of leaves hang like a mobile
from the skinny bole of a beech tree.
They can't help splattering
the face and shoulders of a woman feeding
geese. The woman sits in her dooryard.
The white geese are smooth as soap. A white
    light
accosts them like a breeze. . . .

                         In a field outside
the frame, someone's childhood is taking place.
Imagine the flushed upturned face, the spring
    air
about to break open like an icy fruit, to
run with water and freshness. All glory's
in the weather. In apprehension, not
desire. A consciousness
both rooted and porous, like the memories
of the very old. Somehow
one turns into the other . . . The dots of
the photograph reassemble
by softening. Dusk
swarms above the field. It is possible

to head aimlessly for home. As you walk, something
     out
there grows regular as a heartbeat, the hush
in which night grows audible.

The white geese can be seen from a distance;
the sound in the leaves is voluptuous, forgetful.

AUGUST

In light, hazy as a swarm of gnats, the low hills
come and go. The woman in the yard
looks at the book on her lap, and then at the fields:
slowly the wheat
draws up its sweaty knees. The swallows glide and inhale.
Glide and inhale.

The woman dangles her hand, letting it touch the grass,
but doesn't close her eyes.
The flat leaves dangle from the birches
like chimes.
The sound they make is both rough and tender, like the tongue
of an animal. It reminds her
of something she will know. She feels restless and assured.

Heat glazes the sky. The few clouds
are disappearing
in their places,
carefully and over time, blurring to a standstill
like desire. Like the after-image caused by staring. . . .

Balance is only rhythm, the swing
in the swing
of the pendulum;
neither loss nor possession:

All day the day going backwards like the sea,
the water curling around her feet, and the water
eye-level, a moving desert.

BROWN SUNDAY

Brown as weak tea (the jostling
rings of light just below
its surface) the light lies
as inadvertent as a strand of
hair across one's face, on tree
limbs, fields, flat housefronts,
all lengthened & composed as their
reflections in water

The whole month is still
as Sunday, the same
odd combination of gravity
& abandon, stalled expectation

The awkwardness of failure
of badly managed time is
camouflaged or elevated by
the larger vagueness outside

(the fields behind the house
for instance
without destination though
reverberant as a room in
which a solitary has just
spoken a single word aloud)

November is anomalous, as
elegant stuttering would
be, as loss asking for more:
the flat earth upheld like
the palm of a hand to wide air

JEANNE

for Karen Fish

In the bare field
the trees stood
with their mouths open

to the light
that paused along the ground
like an animal grazing.

I heard the stutter
of pigeons' wings
above my head, the hair

on my wrist bone
grew bright.
When it was over, I wept

and would gladly
have gone with him—
what is desire, but the eye

posthumous?
Now my body aches
from the damp

that I must wear
like another kind of armor
when the flames they speak to me.

JAPANESE

Winter branches
tipped with birds,
fat buds
that blossom on the air;
gray flames
at rest on a poplar
candelabrum;
four—no, three—notes
on a staff:

We hold what solaces
in place
like a fan before the face.

PART TWO

A DAY IN THE NORTH

Spring is triggered. Chartreuse
filigree of tight buds on trees. Low skies.
The tension of delicacy. One bird
losing and recovering its song.
Many different colors of gray.
(This air light as a glance, sharp as a flame.)
New distances. Dust and rain.
The loneliness of the world freshened.

A Painting by Vermeer

for Ralph Zannoni

It is like spring water,
cold   flowing   steady   & clear—
a freshet of light filling the room.
Near the window a woman is pouring
milk into a bowl, passive as a madonna
or good nurse in her starched collar and cap
folded along her round forehead.
Nothing interrupts.
Decorum is a pause between eye and object,
a kind of dispossession.
Life so composed it's anonymous.
                              You are moved
and consoled by your absence, the canny
refusal: not desire—not
          desire, but patience.
All the time in the world. To have it
by looking away. The pleasure
of stalling pleasure, of outwitting
your own response.

Perfection is only good behavior,
like keeping still: it is the art of privacy.
In the painting she holds her head a little
to one side,
lids downcast, her attention hair-fine, like a note sung
sostenuto

To a Friend

Come into the green
gloaming, these
woods heavy as grapes,
their light as phosphorus.
Here everything is details,
partial, replete. One
loose thread triggering
another, the paths you
take are like thought.
No foreground, no background,
just spaces between. Perspective
is a frond in the weave.

Come and disappear
among so much presence, layers
of loss which here and there
consolidate to white
trillium, the tiny green-tinged
tags that pass for flowers along
the broad bent leaf of Solomon's
seal, or the prehistoric
wild ginger whose pan-shaped
leaves, clumsy as fins, hide
the nuzzling brown-red flower.

Whatever falls here
becomes a fetish
in an instant or an age.
In the woods death
is salvaged, woven
into identities fine
as a strand of hair—rock
cress, columbine, the springy
shadow-fed mosses lodged
beneath a spray of ferns.

All these are distractions,
radiating spokes that
draw attention further in.

Come—where Daphne roamed,
not for love, but to be taken
by surprise, an odor swift
interiorizing, one chamber
door after another flung open—
traversed, the sanctum grazed as
you come to, remembering. Transformed
the duration of wet balsam, crushed
        mint.

STILL LIFE FOR BREAKFAST

A plate of citrons, a basket
of oranges, a china cup of water, and a rose
in profile on a pewter saucer: the rigors of decor
preserve us somehow. Take this

still-life whose progress along this table
is as measured and as prickly as the faint-
inked
signature of someone long dead and unknown:
what does it offer? Some combination

of coziness and deprivation, like having
only one of anything—one place setting, one
view—*alone*
in a circle of friends aware of one's loneliness,
the poet's dream of domesticity come true.

And yet in these objects there is
also a quality of great momentum and
arrest:
the paradox of metamorphosis.
Looked at long enough, they record

the mesmeric minute before knowing
in which the slice of water
seems to be (or has just stopped) quivering
in its cup, the delicate rose staring
    sideways
like the eye of a doe. —Sideways

    like surprise,
a true feature of the spiritual life.

(Is there restfulness in deep surprise
—surprise at the bottom of rest?)

Hidden snake-like in every bouquet of fruit
    and timelessness.

WEATHER IN A VASE

The tulips in throes—
                              ducking   craning
    wandering   bowing
from the waist or just lolling around
like the tongue of a madperson
before heaving themselves carefully
                                        overboard.

The vegetable-thick green leaves
have a sudden-found aversion
to the stem—peeling   turning   swimming
away from it. They're fluted as the hands

of a Balinese dancer. These

tulips are more changeable than weather.
They have the border color
of something washed too many times,
the variations in hue of someone
changing altitudes, working
progressively harder to breathe. Once

they were deep rose. Now
they bring to mind a watermelon

stump, the density of juices sucked
away. They ought to make space

intelligible, but they're hard to
read, tortured and decorous as a
monk's script. Their flower
heads are caving in like the silks
of a landed parachute. They've kept
the charming long necks of demoiselles

in distress, those traditional objects
of analogy and demolition.

TREETOPS

The leaves the mad leaves
bucking the light that flickers
and snaps its tentacles across
the back lawn against the house
side struggle   to breach the waves
   of autumn air

They are the dredge—old boot
and rotten stick—that ride
the lip of a whirlpool that
feel the suck of what is to come

ON THE WAY TO TELL MY SISTER

When you were one hour out
of this world
swallows were sailing mightily in the faint
sky.
You were strong then and could have
been anywhere:
in the light-translucent grass,
in the new leaves curled tightly like an infant's
fist. For a while
the things of this world seemed
otherworldly, as if about to rise or speak.
The trees up ahead kept moving
but like flames in sunlight, drawing us on
in the way of the almost-seen. Maybe,
because I hadn't seen you for years, the fact
of your death began as something ingenious, fresh—
it was, for a while, what they say first
love is like: no matter where you are,
being utterly alone with the one you love
and the beautiful things of this world.

WHERE

You're three weeks gone. All
the traveling you'll do now
will be measured by time, not space.
Yet I think of you as someone swimming
across wide water, farther and farther
off shore

> The sea is a blank en masse, a gray
> entablature; at one end, endless sound,
> at the other, the deafening horizon

—so flat, so chalk-bright a line, it seems
on the verge of both appearing and disappearing,

the beachgoer's
daylong sensation of time evaded and intensified.

I'll tell you what it's like. It's like
standing in a rowboat, sighting a wave
far out as it detaches itself, moving
as if on gliders to a point midway
where it runs out—over and over again

while the distance between us grows
steady as the moment of regard.

PORTRAIT OF THE ARTIST

The blonde moon grows whiter
as it rises in the spring sky
which is delicate as a watercolor.
Spring is late this year.
I notice the first leaves growing
in curly on the shorn branches poised
as sprigs. For a while, they garnish
the moon. For a while, the difference
between foreground and background is
most obvious as that between the dark
loaded hills and faint sky. I love
the moment of contrast—though
it's hard to achieve: enough loss to
provoke the sharpness of detail; enough
content to sleep by my lover all night.

PART THREE

VESPERS

The birds are telling of
    recesses in the air, of near
invisible thickets, long damp
corridors they go back and forth
on. The sound is telescopic—both
ends—minnow-quick and sly as sunlight
ricocheting off the bored one's knife-
    blade.
Listen. Lost and found is a baroque
affair. Intricate, intrinsic and
progressive. The way out of the forest
reappears but only up ahead.

PERSEPHONE

for my mother

1

Light stuttering
over the field, the scrawny
haunches of those hills
brown and shivering
as though the sky
had overturned above them;
the air wobbly,
damp as the underside of a rock

Raw spring: when overnight the world
is intimate, incoherent
like a face close up, a detail

isolate/shiny/hidden

. . . To go under
and return without memory

to the same place;
the glamour

of a rest
from experience, of

metamorphosis—

2

Though in the upper world
the atmosphere is all
vitality and amputation, here
it's loosely packed, moveable
yet undisturbed

Sometimes it's like walking
in your own house late
at night with a glass from
room to room, calmly thinking

Or it resembles dread
Often I can't tell whether
something important is
about to happen or already has

I think we forget
in order to have something,
the same pressure
of unknowing we felt on earth

Our past lives are buried
to give eternity depth

3

We walked
through the cold clear autumn wet,
the sky a fluctuant blue flame, the clouds
shouldering light that now and then spilled
rippling like a loosened braid.
                              Above our heads
migrating blackbirds tossed and pitched like fleets
of stiff-prowed ships. As always on a last day
we felt something draw back. Or maybe
       draw closer.
Pristine as a mountaintop when the fogs disperse
and it comes into view, immediate and unapproachable
—whatever changed was like that. Our future
loss experienced as the calm of decision or rest.
Long rest.
                    The beautiful trout-water

brown of the field kept going by us as we passed.
Interrupted at every glance by color so brilliant
       & exhausted
it was an aftermath—nature fairly showing
herself as the exhilaration of having survived life.

For some reason, the way back was always shorter
       or longer than the way out.
The two are inseparable though never the same.
Like vision, which is always part fulfillment, part
delay.

THE ODYSSEY

After graduating from college, Chris McCandless donated the remainder of his tuition fund, over $24,000, to OXFAM to fight hunger. For two years he traveled alone across the country and up and down the continent, living the self-reliant life. Finally, he decided to begin his "odyssey," journeying to Alaska in order to fulfill his goal of being "lost in the wild." Less than four months after his arrival there, Chris died of starvation. The police who read the notebooks next to his body thought he was a naturalist. Those who've seen the last photographs Chris took of himself in the wild describe them as joyous.

I put my head down like a bull, a plow, a nun
walking. I could not fool my purpose. *Moose.*
Squirrel. Gold bird. Wildflowers close to
the ground. Their odor of faint, very clean
decay, as though in cool morning air you could
smell the bottom of a pond. O it is a joy

to be hidden, but a disaster not to be found.

Not eating. Not sleeping much. Walking
     around.
The cold when it arrives is both unnerving

and exhilarating, like being responded to
immediately. This afternoon I fell asleep
again and dreamt while I was walking toward
it I saw a tree stand up in the middle of
a field—Day 105: I've had a happy life—
think of all that I can think and see yet
on my way there.

ORPHEUS AND EURYDICE TAKE A WALK

for Aida Khalil

I would go for a walk every day.
Just before the sun began
to pick up speed going down, or
just after the hour it had risen.
At sunset the light was low and steady:
it could be followed to its source.
But like a spill the morning light
was out of reach and everywhere at once.
I would walk up the field to the hill
and then, more slowly,
back down.
The morning air and the morning light
were the same thing. I'd watch them
in the evenings come apart:

Color deserts the field slowly, traveling
up like a ghost.
What the trees lose in color, they gain
in mass. And the hills
also, coming together like a furrowed brow.
Everywhere form spreading like feeling . . .

I saw the light turn to look behind him;
the earth went backward like a sigh,

a low whistle—

        amor

fati, the invisible smoke of memory loved
without dread or sensuality: the body
rooted and moving, the unfinished
the unfinished as eternal,
sorrow like two hands smoothing one's hair.

Above the cold marine horizon
the first slippery star would appear.

SIMONE WEIL IN THE BATH

Spring 1937, 1938

Think how your cheekbone feels
to the palm of your hand after
you've been outdoors, the flesh
fleshier, riper somehow for being
chilled

How strange comfort is   At dusk
the spring air is like water,
in places suddenly deeper, colder

Dusk   the violet countdown
at which the horizon
burns greener than a peeled twig

At Santa Maria degli Angeli something
stronger than myself forced me to
my knees

Think of the chapel as a hollow
nest swaying, a provincialism
like the shove a peasant gives
the earth each spring

when the bandages of cold have
been removed & the countryside
appears shrunken, derelict   *I*

was able to rise above this
wretched flesh, to leave it
by itself heaped in a corner

& find a pure and perfect joy
in being devoured invisibly

Think how still humility is,
how comforting to desire,
as though a light rain fell
regularly, here & in the distance

"HEAD OF A YOUNG GIRL"

(Vermeer)

If Christ had hung his eyes
on the watery sun or desert
heat shimmering in the flat
distance; if his gaze had
strayed to the wood sweating
salt grains of light, or caught
like briar on the vague blue of
Mary's skirt, making of that hem
a fluctuant horizon . . .

How much harder it is to die
when subject
to that fierce rein and tether of the eye.

STILL LIFE OF THE MARTYRDOM OF ST. SERAPION

for Edward Ruchalski

Slow

        Slow

                Slowed
as a mote in a shaft of sunlight,
   St. Serapion lists
to his right; the ropes pulling
each arm away from his body and above
his head have been relaxed, slightly.
                They could be

stage ropes, props; it's hard to see. The black
background is dark
as a shovelful of earth. Though on the saint's
white robes a light pauses like the highlight
                on a pearl.

How long the moment is, and how imminent.
   Like a tear
welling in the eye and still remaining there.
             Is he dead

   or asleep?

His robes are heavy as sleep. And complicated
as machinery. Their complexity
a form of reticence to help the viewer imagine

                                                    pain.

Of the two ways to pray—one, full of unknowing
tenderness, the other
chronic and dry as a cough in the chest—

                                          which

leads here, where the light rests
       —not
on the face, but—exclusive and engrossed
on a dead hand

                     whose wrinkled shirt-cuff seems

to say, the familiar is the true mysterious?

Is the steadiness we feel
       dread, or the pressure of hope held
back like a laugh?

WHAT FIERY EYE

The font of crisis or sensation
on whose jet this lark borne
upward rests teetering
over a wheatfield has long since
subsided, a figment of memory &
weather.

As if on a double-dare, a wish
for serenity rather than for
strangeness, Van Gogh went
south, following the dream
of a well-tempered temperament
produced he thought by
steady heat, wind, the cicada
shivering somewhere out of sight.

Painting infinity, whatever
dies because it is not dying
beneath the sun—iris, herds
of corn, wheat, the flat
horizons of Le Crau
which like a great technique
at once suggest & betray all
hope for a beyond—he saw too
clearly.

High-minded, lonely, after 6
months forestalling company &
repose, he refashioned himself
for Gauguin as a Japanese
monk in whose pressed features
& close-shaven head uncanniness
vies with shame.

At 37 having suffered all
over again the dispersion
of spring, autumns
fogged by misgivings in another
climate, he wrote his
brother a last time in fatigue:

"But what do you want?"

Not a house, nor a garden; not
children. Opportunities
are vulgar. Give me, a 3rd wind.

HOMAGE TO THE FIELDS AND HILLS
WHICH ARE MY BACKYARD

When I go there
from all sides
my dead dreams
rise to greet me
like flames stretching
in the wind:

There you are
There you are

The stiffness goes
out of me like
mercury
from a glass. It
lodges in my feet
and the dear earth
under them—
an intimacy accorded
by gravity,
so that
I too begin to sway.
All rooted things sway.

ELEVEN DAYS BEFORE SPRING

To the memory of Jeremy Lake

There's been a flood overnight, the tide
that always recedes by morning
was here.
What is the difference, I wonder,
between drowning and total immersion? Which one
means surrender, to respond without commotion?

The long field is strewn with newly visible debris.
The bare trees look naked and remote. Like
Daphne, the moment she raised her arms
above her head, mocking the attitude of surrender.

Surrender. The wave draws back   draws back
    like a bow.
The disappearing   circles

of calm   come later. The other bodies lying
on the field crooked as trees, and the trees
dotting the countryside like survivors
wandering and dazed
by the fact of their surviving. They know
all history as surrender: the fame of loss and

return.

Eleven days before spring. Anticipation
is the marriage of time to pleasure—the geese
that are somewhere overhead, much louder than
they are near, and already far off when I see
them—a moving line of scribble on course. On
course and distracted. Alone with their instinct
and the sky.

                    The isolate

dissolving perception, like a place cut off
by water, an ice floe, one thought's exile from another—
To run thinking though not for long:

The air is melting. The light has a body.

NOTES

The line in italics in the poem "Still Life for Breakfast" is from *The Burning Brand: Diaries 1935–1950,* by Cesare Pavese (New York: Walker, 1961).

The poem "The Odyssey" was inspired by an article by Chip Brown published in *The New Yorker.*

The italicized lines in the poem "Simone Weil in the Bath" are slightly paraphrased from "Simone Weil's Spiritual Autobiography" in *The Simone Weil Reader,* edited by George A. Panichas (New York: David McKay Company, 1977).